JUNGLE OF FEAR
TUNNEL OF DOUBT
ICY CLIFFS
FROZEN
OCEAN

KORVAX THE SEA DRAGON

BY ADAM BLADE

DRAKONIA
WELL OF POWER
PLAIN OF BONES
PORTAL OF FIRE
LAVA SEA
BLACK MOUNTAINS

WELCOME TO

Collect the special coins in this book. You will earn one gold coin for every chapter you read.

Once you have finished all the chapters, find out what [illegible] your gold coins at the ba[illegible]

With special thanks to Allan Frewin Jones

For Casey Ray Bush

www.beastquest.co.uk

ORCHARD BOOKS

First published in Great Britain in 2017 by The Watts Publishing Group

1 3 5 7 9 10 8 6 4 2

A CIP catalogue record for this book is available from the British Library.

ISBN 978 1 40834 313 5

Printed and bound by CPI Group (UK) Ltd, Croydon, CR0 4YY

The paper and board used in this book are made from wood from responsible sources.

Orchard Books
An imprint of Hachette Children's Group
Part of The Watts Publishing Group Limited
Carmelite House, 50 Victoria Embankment, London EC4Y 0DZ

An Hachette UK Company
www.hachette.co.uk
www.hachettechildrens.co.uk

CONTENTS

When I was a young apprentice wizard, there was a secret chamber my master forbade me to enter. But even then, I did not like being told what to do. With a simple unlocking spell, I found my way in.

I was very disappointed. For that room contained no potions or poisons, no magical weapons. All I saw was a single oval stone, grey and speckled, lying on a cushion.

My master found me. To my surprise, he did not beat or curse me. Instead he smiled.

"Jezrin," he said, "behold the key to immeasurable power!"

"What, an old rock?" I replied.

At that, his face turned grave. "That is no rock, apprentice. That is a dragon egg. And one day it will allow you to spread Evil to every corner of every kingdom."

As he led me from the room, I was not impressed. My master never lived to see the egg hatch. But his promise proved true.

The time of Evil has come. And nothing – no one – can stand in my path.

THE SNOWLANDS

Tom stood on a barren hilltop, gazing across the kingdom of Drakonia. All around him, volcanoes spewed smoke into the sky, and rivers of lava trailed down rocky mountains. Using the power of the golden helmet, Tom scanned far into the distance.

"There's no sign of Jezrin," he said, sighing.

Petra placed her hands on her hips. The witch's red crow, Rourke, squawked on her shoulder. "Either he's using magic to hide from you, or he cast a speed spell," Petra said. "Either way, he's heading for the Well of Power."

"Maybe Berric knows which way he went," said Elenna.

Tom turned to the stone figure of Jezrin's apprentice, hands frozen over his face. Under the Evil Wizard's control, the dragon Quarg had encased Berric in a layer of rock.

"He would never tell," said Tom,

shaking his head. "And we can't waste time trying to free him." He sat down on a boulder, worry churning in his stomach. "The moment Jezrin drinks from the well, he'll become invincible," he said.

"Well, obviously, I could always track him," said Petra, feeding a bit of stale bread to Rourke.

Elenna raised her eyebrows. "Why didn't you say that before?"

Petra shrugged. "You didn't ask."

"How can you?" said Tom, urgently.

"Every wizard leaves a trail on the air when using magic," said Petra. She wrinkled her nose. "Jezrin's scent is most powerful. I could smell him two kingdoms away! Sulphur, boiled cabbage and bad feet."

Elenna grimaced. "Rather you than me," she muttered.

"Then your nose can guide us," Tom said to Petra. He led them down the hilltop to where Ferno lay waiting. The great fire dragon's wings were folded along his ridged back, his scales reflecting the red glow of the volcanoes. Drakonia was the kingdom where all dragons came from, and only dragons knew how to cross into the realm. Jezrin and Berric had used Quarg, and Tom had summoned the Good Beast Ferno to carry them there.

Tom climbed on to the Beast's back

and spoke to him through the red jewel of Torgor. *We need your help again, old friend.*

Petra and Elenna settled

themselves between Ferno's spiny ridges. The witch sat up, sniffing.

"Jezrin went that way," she said, pointing north.

"North, Ferno!" Tom commanded. The huge Beast rose to his feet and spread his wings. Tom felt a rush of air on his face as the dragon leaped high, wings beating steadily as he carried them above the hills.

On they flew, passing beyond the land of volcanoes until they soared over mountains whose foothills were dusted with snow. The air became cold, and although the fire dragon's body was warm beneath them, Tom could see his breath gusting white as they sped along. He turned to Petra. Rourke still clung to her shoulder, the wind ruffling his red feathers.

"One thing puzzles me," Tom said. "How did Jezrin first gain control of Quarg?"

"It's said that Jezrin's master stole a dragon's egg from Drakonia," Petra replied. "Jezrin raised Quarg from a hatchling."

"That would make it far easier for him to control the poor Beast," said Elenna thoughtfully.

Petra raised her chin and sniffed. "Jezrin's close," she said.

Tom guided Ferno lower, soaring

through a low valley. Tom scanned the ground rushing past beneath him. He spied a line of marks in the snow. "Footprints!" he cried. "They're man-sized. But they're too far apart."

"Jezrin is using a leaping spell," said Petra, squinting at the prints.

Elenna grinned. "He's still not as fast as a dragon, though."

Just then, Tom felt Ferno shudder beneath him as the fire dragon's wings faltered.

"I think you spoke too soon," said Petra.

Tom felt a rush of worry for his old friend. *Something's wrong*.

"Is it the cold?" asked Elenna, as Ferno struggled along, dipping lower at every wingbeat.

"He might be tired," Tom said. "It's been a long flight with no rest."

It is more than tiredness, said Ferno, in Tom's head. *My wings feel leaden and my heart labours. Some dark magic is working against me.*

Set us down now, said Tom. *We can't let you get hurt.*

Tom clung on grimly as the ground raced up to meet them. Ferno's great back arched, and his wings spread back. But the dragon wobbled in the air, and they hit the ground hard, the dragon's forelegs collapsing beneath him. Snow and ice gushed into Tom's face, blinding him. He could hear Elenna and Petra yelling in alarm as

Ferno bumped along the valley floor.

At last, he slithered to a stop in a deep trough of snow.

Tom wiped his eyes as Ferno rose to his feet. His great body shuddered as he lifted his head and shook the

snow off his scales.

"Quite a ride!" Petra gasped. "I thought we were done for!"

"Ferno would never let us come to harm," said Elenna.

Tom climbed down and waded

through shin-deep snow to Ferno's head. *You've done well, old friend*, he said through the jewel. *You should head back to Avantia.*

Ferno's voice growled in his mind. *I will not abandon you here. You are unsafe in this land of dragons.*

We'll be fine, Tom insisted. *Avantia is your home now. The realm needs you. Go now, with my thanks.*

Ferno nodded and sprang into the air. Tom could see how the Good Beast struggled to beat his great wings as he turned and headed south. Tom hoped Ferno would feel stronger as he left Drakonia's skies.

"Well, this is fun," muttered Petra, pulling her cloak tight. "If you like snow. Which I don't."

Tom gazed around. The peaks of the narrow valley reared up either side of them. Long cracks threaded along the ground. Tom found Jezrin's trail. "Let's go," he said. "Jezrin can't be far away." As Tom led the others forwards, the ground shuddered under his feet, giving out low creaks and groans.

"Great," said Petra. "We're going to get swallowed by an earthquake."

"At least it will put an end to your moaning," muttered Elenna.

They followed the footprints up the hillside, each stride twice as long as Tom was tall. He watched uneasily as avalanches tumbled down distant mountainsides with deep rumbles.

They clambered to the peak and stared down in amazement at a vast sea of dark blue water. Jagged icebergs drifted on the waves.

"I had no idea we were near the coast," Tom said. He spied Jezrin's trail leaping down the slope towards the shore. "Come on!" He took a step forwards.

The ground gave way beneath his foot.

Tom cried out as he plunged straight downwards. He heard flapping wings, and spotted Rourke lifting off Petra's shoulder. The witch and Elenna fell through the air beside him. Snow and ice obscured

Tom's vision as they dropped into a sheer chasm.

THE ICE TRAP

Tom reached out with his hands, but there was nothing to get a grip on.

Thud! The air rushed from his lungs as he slammed to a sudden stop, buried in white powder. Elenna crashed down next to him, followed by Petra, landing face-first with a muffled shriek.

The sky was just a grey patch,

high above. Tom realised they hadn't fallen far. They were in the bottom of a crevasse – a deep hole in the ice. His body trembled, but he took a calming breath. It could have been a lot worse.

Elenna helped Petra to her feet. The witch clawed snow off her face. "Did I mention I hate snow?" she grumbled. She glared at Tom. "Now what?"

'We climb out," Tom said, scanning the mouth of the crevasse. Then he noticed something odd. Thick strands of woven reed hung down from the edges of the opening.

"That isn't natural," he said, pointing up. "We're in some kind of

man-made trap."

"Yes, I see," said Elenna. "The reeds form a thin, hidden layer under the snow – and the moment you step on it, they give way." She frowned. "Jezrin wouldn't have had time to dig this out."

"It's not his style, anyway," said Petra. "If he set a trap, it would be something nastier than a hole in the ice."

Tom examined the ice walls – sheer and smooth, without any handholds. "I could use my golden boots to leap out, but you two would still be stuck," said Tom.

"I could try magic fire to burn steps in the ice," Petra suggested. "But it might cause the whole thing to collapse."

"It may be safer if I hack out hand and foot holds with my sword," said Tom. "But it will take a while." *Every moment we waste means Jezrin is getting further ahead of us.*

"Then get hacking," said Petra, hugging herself against the cold.

Tom was about to draw his sword when he heard the sound of voices above him.

"It's probably just a snow-bear," said a gruff voice.

"Hey!" Tom shouted up. "We stumbled into your trap by accident."

Tom heard a hiss; then there was a short silence before five heads appeared, dark against the sky.

The people that peered down at them were clad in thick skins and had fur hats on their heads. Tom gasped, seeing that their faces were covered in bluish scales, like reptiles. He had never seen anything like it.

"You're the expert on Drakonia," hissed Elenna to Petra. "You didn't tell us lizard people lived here."

"You didn't ask," the witch

whispered back.

Two of the people leaned further out, and Tom saw that they held crossbows.

"Their skin is smooth!" said the one with the gruff voice. "How ugly!"

"Shoot them, Vax, and be done," growled another of the people.

"No, Nordo,"Vax replied. "They must give us information first." He leaned even further out. "What have you done with Simeon? Speak swiftly, or die!"

"We don't know what you mean," Tom called up.

"We've never heard of anyone called Simeon," added Elenna.

"Despicable liars!" hissed one of the crossbow-wielding men.

"Do not seek to fool us with your tricks!" snarled Vax. "Simeon is my son. He has gone missing and it is no accident that you three should appear at the same time!" His voice rose to an angry screech. "What have you done with him?"

"We're strangers from Avantia," called Tom. "We mean no harm. We don't know anything about..."

"Avantia!" howled Vax. "Only thieves and liars come from that kingdom." The eyes of the strange people blazed with anger.

"Listen, please," called Elenna. "We're on an important mission. You must help us."

"We shall pin you to the ice with

a thousand barbs!" spat Nordo. Tom saw crossbows being levelled.

"Listen to us," called Petra. "An Evil Wizard called Jezrin has come to your realm to cause trouble."

"Free us and we'll find Jezrin and stop him," Tom cried.

"If this wizard exists, we will deal with him," growled Vax. "You repulsive creatures can remain in the pit until you freeze to death." His voice rose again. "Your only hope is to tell us what you did with Simeon!"

Petra sighed. "I've had enough of this nonsense," she muttered. The witch tilted her head up, and closed her eyes halfway.

"What's she doing?" muttered Elenna.

Moments later, Tom heard a harsh squawk from above. He saw a dark shape fly into Vax's face. Petra had summoned Rourke! The lizard man staggered back with his hands up to his eyes as the red crow clawed at him.

The other men shouted and sprang towards Vax, but before they could reach him, Vax's foot slipped on the edge of the pit and he tumbled over. Tom leaped back as the lizard man crashed at his feet in a flurry of snow.

Tom whipped his sword out and brought the tip of the blade to Vax's

throat before the reptile man could get to his feet. "Stay perfectly still," he ordered. He had no intention of harming the man, but Vax and his companions didn't know that. Vax hissed with hatred.

"Drop your weapons into the pit," Tom shouted up to the other scaled men. "Then throw down a rope so we can climb out. Or your leader dies!"

The lizard men gathered together, muttering angrily. Nordo came to the edge and flung the crossbows down. Then he unreeled a coil of thick rope.

"You go first," Tom told Elenna and Petra. They climbed the rope and clambered out of the pit. Tom followed, the power of the Golden Armour allowing him to climb the rope in seconds.

At the top, Rourke landed on Petra's shoulder, watching the lizard men intently. Elenna had notched an arrow and aimed it at the one called Nordo. Tom drew his sword.

"Come up now," he called to Vax.

The reptile man climbed up and stood in front of Tom, bristling with fury.

"Where did your son go missing?" Tom asked calmly.

"By the shore!" said Vax, pointing towards the frozen sea. "As if you didn't know!"

"We just want to be left to fulfil our Quest," said Elenna.

"Go then, with my curses on you," snarled Vax. He pointed a finger in Tom's face. "If we cross paths again, it will be as mortal enemies."

Tom turned, trudging away through the snow with Petra and Elenna.

Petra let out a low whistle. "I think we've made a friend there," she said.

Tom sighed. Vax's son might have had an accident, but it was more likely that Jezrin was involved in his disappearance. Either way, they had wasted far too much time here. For all Tom knew, Jezrin could already be drinking from the Well of Power!

1

DEATHLY BLIZZARD

Tom led his companions down the snowy hillside. A bitter wind blew over the restless waters. Icebergs rose and fell on the churning waves. Elenna stood at the water's edge, her breath like a gush of fog.

"We're not dressed for this weather,"Tom said. He knew that the bell of Nanook, embedded in

his shield, was helping him fight the cold, but the faces of the two girls were blueish and Petra's teeth were chattering.

He gazed anxiously up the long hillside. *What if Vax goes for reinforcements? We can't hold off a whole tribe.*

"I don't see any sign of the missing boy," Tom said, scanning the length of the shoreline, the power of the golden helmet revealing every tiny detail to him. "Do you think Jezrin had anything to do with his disappearance?" asked Elenna.

"Count on it," said Petra. "But he wouldn't snatch a child for no reason. Mark my words, it'll be part of some bigger plan."

"Look for footprints or any signs of a scuffle," said Tom, walking along the shore. "We need to know which way they went."

"Not that way, I hope," said

Elenna, pointing to a series of black holes in the hillside. "Vax mentioned snow-bears. Those caves are perfect lairs for animals." She frowned. "Might Simeon have been attacked by a bear?"

"I haven't seen any sign of blood," said Tom.

"Perhaps I can change that for you," sneered a voice. Tom spun around, drawing his sword.

Jezrin stood a little way along the beach. The wizard's haughty eyes regarded them with amusement, his dark cloak folded around his body, his hair and beard blowing in the wind.

"Welcome to the frost-lands of

Drakonia," Jezrin jeered. "I hope you're keeping warm. I would hate for the cold to kill you before I do."

Tom stepped forwards, his sword pointed at the wizard's heart. "Your taunts don't impress me, Jezrin," he said. "What have you done with the boy?"

Jezrin grinned. "I knew you wouldn't be able to resist playing the hero again. It's not a good idea, wandering the coast of these seas. They can be deadly..."

Elenna took an arrow from her quiver and aimed it at the wizard. "I've had enough of your hot air!"

Jezrin laughed. "Then try some truly cold air!" he said, raising his arms and twirling his hands. Blizzards surged from his palms, hurtling at them, spitting snow into their faces.

Tom raised his shield as the icy wind smashed into him. The force

pushed him back, sliding on the ice. He held his shield firm and managed to dig in his feet, but saw with horror that Petra and Elenna were being driven towards the sea.

Elenna fired an arrow, but the wind spun the shaft around so it flew straight back at her.

Tom lunged sideways, reaching out with his shield. The arrow thudded into the wood. Snow and ice were clogging his eyes, filling his hair and stinging his face. He couldn't even make out the wizard through the bitter onslaught.

We have to get out of here, or we'll freeze to death!

"Follow me!" he howled against

the shriek of the blizzard. He struggled along the beach, using his shield to keep off the worst of the snowstorm. "To the caves!"

Petra and Elenna pressed close behind him as they forced their way up the beach. Tom was almost torn off his feet, but now could see the black mouth of a cave.

A few desperate moments later, the three of them tumbled into the cave. The storm lashed at the hillside, but here they were safe from its fury.

"Have I told you that I hate snow?" said Petra, brushing ice and white powder off herself.

Elenna turned to the cave mouth. "There's no sign of Jezrin," she gasped. "I don't think he's coming for us."

Tom took a breath, wiped ice off his face and looked around, relieved that there was no sign of bears.

The cave tunnelled deep into the hillside, curving through the brown rock. There was enough light for him to see paintings on the walls. They showed dragons flying over a raging sea.

"These look very old," Tom said.

"What do you think they mean?" asked Elenna.

Tom shook his head. "I don't know."

"I don't like it," said Petra. "Dragons are never good news." She peered deeper into the cave. "I see light down there," she said. "And the air feels warmer."

Tom and Elenna joined the witch as she made her way along the curved tunnel.

Flickering firelight played on the walls ahead of them.

"I smell cooking!" said Elenna.

Tom sniffed. *Yes!* There was a rich scent of stew on the air, making his mouth water.

They rounded a shoulder of rock and found themselves in a great cavern lit by a roaring fire. A small group of people sat around it on reed mats, dressed in furs and eating from wooden bowls. Animal skins hung from the walls. Tom stepped forward and blue-scaled faces turned to him in fear. Some of the men leaped up, reaching for knives and clubs.

Tom sheathed his sword, not wanting to alarm them. He held out

his arms. "We come in peace," he called.

An elderly woman stood up and stared at Tom and Elenna with twinkling, intelligent eyes. "Lay down your weapons," she commanded the men.

Tom was relieved to see that they obeyed her without question, although they kept their eyes fixed on Tom and his companions. Was this woman their leader, perhaps?

"Come," she said, beckoning to them. "You look half dead with cold. Eat with us and be warmed at our fireside."

"Do we trust them?" whispered Petra. Rourke squawked on her

shoulder, and Petra stroked his feathers.

"They seem peaceful," replied Tom. "Thank you," he said to the elderly lizard woman, and he sat down by the fire.

Elenna, and then Petra, eased themselves down next to him. They were given hot bowls of fish stew, thick and tasty. Tom felt the warmth seeping into his limbs.

"Forgive my people for drawing weapons on you," said the old woman. "We are sad and wary. One of our children is missing, and we fear the worst."

"We met with some of your folk," said Tom. "We were told about

Simeon. You have our sympathy." He left out that Vax and his men had wanted to turn them into human pincushions with their crossbows.

The woman nodded her gratitude.

"We saw the cave paintings back there," said Elenna. "Were they made by your people?"

"They were painted long ago to revere the great Beast we fear and honour," explained the old woman while the others looked on with watchful eyes. "Her name is Korvax, meaning 'ice-wings', and she is ancient beyond telling. But she does us no harm so long as we keep away from the deep of the sea."

Tom's eyes widened. Jezrin's tracks had led to that sea. Was he looking for the Beast?

The lizard woman looked at them. "You are not the first of your kind I've seen," she said. "A wizard came from a land called Avantia...when I was only a small girl."

Tom's ears pricked up at this. "Do you remember anything about him?" he asked.

The old woman nodded. "He sought dragon eggs," she said.

She's speaking of Jezrin's master!

Tom was about to ask more, when he heard footsteps echoing along the tunnel.

Five reptile men appeared, clad in furs, two of them carrying crossbows.

"Uh-oh!" said Petra.

Tom scrambled to his feet as he recognised the small band who had set the trap in the ice. They had retrieved their weapons from the pit.

Vax's eyes blazed in anger and he pulled a knife from his belt. "How do you dare to come here?" he shouted.

Nordo drew an axe, and the others aimed their crossbows. Vax ran straight towards Tom, holding the knife high.

THE FROZEN HORROR

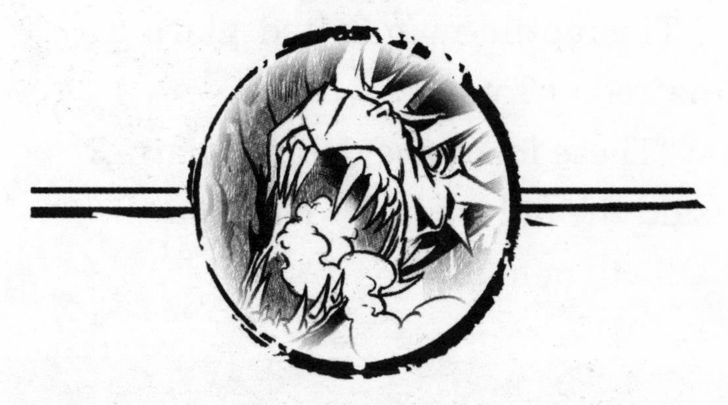

Tom drew his sword, but Elenna leaped in from the side, bringing her bow down on Vax's wrist. The knife dropped from his fingers. The lizard man elbowed her aside, his face red with rage. He paced towards Tom.

Tom took a step back, unwilling to use his sword on an unarmed man.

"Cease this strife!" cried the old woman, stepping between Tom and the charging Vax.

The reptile-man halted, glaring hatred at Tom.

"These folk have done no harm," said the old woman. "They may be able to help us."

"They are strangers," snarled Vax. "They cannot be trusted! They could have taken Simeon."

"We know who took the boy!" said Tom. "It was Jezrin, an Evil Wizard from Avantia."

The old lizard woman looked shocked, and was about to reply when a terrible, high-pitched shriek echoed down the tunnel. It shook the ground under Tom's feet.

"That's the voice of a Beast!" he cried, striding towards the entrance of the cave.

"Do not go out there," warned the scaled woman. "When the dragon comes, we must hide."

"I fear no Beast," said Tom. He

looked at Petra and Elenna. "We saw Jezrin by the coast where the Beast is. Korvax may hold the key to this Quest. We have to confront her." He raced down the tunnel, flanked by Petra and Elenna, while Rourke flew above Petra's head.

They came to the entrance to find the world wrapped in a dense, frozen sea mist. Tom stared around, lips and eyelashes freezing instantly.

Aaarriiiiieeeeekkk.

The haunting cry pierced through the mist. Tom spun around, the hilt of his sword like an icicle in his fist. The terrifying screaming seemed to be coming from everywhere.

"Rourke!" called Petra urgently.

"Find the dragon!"

The red crow vanished into the mist. Petra became stiff, her eyes glazing over, taking on a ruby tinge.

She's seeing with the bird's eyes.

At their backs Tom sensed the fear of the lizard-folk waiting just inside the cave.

"Ahhh!" Petra let out a terrified cry, and stumbled back. Tom caught her, stopping her falling. The witch blinked several times then stared at him, fear in her eyes. "She's coming!"

The red crow hurtled through the mist and landed in a flurry of feathers on her shoulder. It let out a single harsh cry as it huddled in terror against Petra's neck.

Tom staggered as a sensation of burning rage knifed into his mind. *The Beast! I feel it through the jewel of Torgor! Such anger and hatred.*

He saw a sinuous shape gliding high in the air, cutting through the icy fog. Its great shadow circled above them like some giant bird of prey. Tom caught a glimpse of huge shining talons, and vast leathery wings. Yellow eyes flashed. Then she was gone again, lost in the fog.

The three of them drew together, Elenna putting an arrow to the string. "I can't see it," she said.

Petra was muttering to herself, while Rourke flapped nervously on her shoulder.

Tom's heart jolted in his chest as the dragon tore suddenly through the clouds. With a flurry of wings she landed on the icy shore in front of them. Korvax's wings rose over her back. The spines between the leathery skin spread like great skeletal fingers. The flesh was ribbed like the fins of some monstrous deep-sea fish. She whipped her long tail, and Tom saw that the end was a barbed, bony fin.

The dragon's head rose on her long neck, jaws stretching open. Tom caught a glimpse of teeth like purple spears. The dragon let out another heart-stopping shriek, her tail slapping the water and sending up fountains of spray.

Icy breath gushed from the dragon's throat. Tom backed away with the others, as he searched for some weakness in the Beast's scaled body. He blinked. "She's made of ice!" he hissed. "Do you see?"

Korvax's razor-sharp scales were

almost see-through, and shimmered as her muscles moved, the colour shifting from glittering black to green, like oil in water. Tom saw creatures frozen inside the dragon's icy flesh – fish and crabs and limpets and squid.

Elenna sent an arrow whizzing at the dragon, and fired a second before the first struck. They dug into Korvax's scales, but the Beast didn't seem to notice.

Tom heard the old woman's urgent voice behind him. "Try this." She and Vax and a couple of others had come from the cave, carrying torches. "Korvax does not like flame."

Elenna dipped an arrow into the flames and as soon as it ignited, she fired. As the flaming arrow sped towards the dragon, the great creature flinched, wings beating, her tail lashing from side to side.

"It's working!" cried Tom. "Try another arrow!"

The Beast edged away, shaking her head and hissing. She reared up, and Tom caught sight of something truly horrible. Embedded in Korvax's flank, trapped under a veil of icy scales, was a boy. His arms stretched out, and a look of terror was frozen on his scaly blue face.

SEA OF DEATH

Korvax spread her wings and leaped into the air, mist rolling over her. She beat her wings, climbing higher. With a final shriek, the dragon vanished into the fog. Vax staggered down the beach.

"Korvax has taken my son!" he wailed.

Tom turned to the old woman. "Do

you have a boat?"

She nodded. "A small vessel for fishing in the shallows," she said. "But we never take it far out to sea for fear of Korvax."

"I have to follow the Beast!" said Tom.

"You're out of your mind," said Petra. "Chasing that dragon across an icy sea? You'll be killed."

"You're coming too," Tom said to her. "We may need Rourke's eyes."

Petra groaned.

Vax strode up to Tom. "I'll come with you. It is my child that Korvax has stolen."

Tom placed a respectful hand on the man's arm. "It's too dangerous," he replied. But he saw the determination in the man's lizard-like eyes. *In his place, I'd feel the same.* "Very well," said Tom.

Vax led them to where a small coracle-like boat lay beached. The frame of the round boat was made of woven wood. Leather strips formed its hull. Tom eyed it doubtfully. *Will such a flimsy craft even bear our weight?*

"It is strong and sturdy, and light on the water," Vax said. He took a lit torch and clambered into the boat.

"No," said Tom, pulling the torch out of his hand. "Korvax will see the flames. If we're to defeat the Beast, we have to take her by surprise."

Vax looked worried as Tom handed the torch back to one of the other men.

"Here," the old woman pushed a flint and some mossy kindling into Elenna's hands, while one of the men gave her lengths of wood with tarred cloth wound around one end. "You can make fire quickly with these."

Vax held the boat steady as Tom and Elenna and Petra climbed aboard.

"This is such a bad idea," murmured Petra as she took a seat in the stern. Rourke clung to her shoulder and stared around with uneasy eyes.

Vax took the oars and rowed away

from the shoreline. Tom stood at the prow, looking into the white mist, his drawn sword in his hand. The only sound Tom could hear was the clanking of the oars in their locks and the swirl of the water. Tom turned to see Elenna making a lasso from the mooring rope.

"You people have the bearing of warriors," said Vax. "Have you faced Beasts before?"

"A few," Tom said.

"He's being modest," said Petra. "He's defeated hundreds of them. I'm amazed he's still alive!"

Vax grunted and rowed further out. Chunks of ice banged against the boat's leather hide as the prow cut through the slush. A huge shape reared up in front of them. It was an iceberg, tall as the walls of an Avantian city. Vax steered and the iceberg glided eerily past. As the mist parted, Tom saw that the high peaks of many more icebergs surrounded them.

Perfect cover for a Beast. Korvax could be anywh—

The waters erupted in front of him, frothing and foaming and spitting out needle-sharp splinters of ice. The dreadful shape of the sea dragon surged into the air.

"Light the torches!" shouted Tom, bracing his legs as the boat rocked.

He heard the sharp clack of flints being struck together behind him.

A moment later Elenna scrambled forwards, brandishing a flaming torch. The Beast gave a bone-chilling screech and plunged towards them. Tom took the torch and thrust it at Korvax.

The dragon's jaws gaped and Tom was driven backwards by a blast of frozen air. For a moment he lost his balance in the lurching boat. The torch flickered in his hand, his fingers numbed.

He could see the flame reflected in the Beast's pale, cold eyes.

Korvax reared up, avoiding the flames. Tom let out a gasp, ducking to avoid the raking claws. *Too close!* With a cry, Elenna swung the lasso and let it loose. Tom held his breath as he watched the rope snake through the air. Would it work?

At the very last moment, the loop

caught around Korvax's tail as it flicked past. The rope tightened. Elenna was almost wrenched off her feet, but she managed to loop the end of the rope over a jutting wooden spar in the boat. The vessel bucked and tipped, water pouring over the sides.

"Korvax will drown us all!" cried Vax.

"I won't let that happen!" shouted Tom, clinging to the sides of the boat. "Give me the oars!"

The rope stretched taut as the Beast dragged the boat around and towed it further out to sea.

Tom could hardly see for flying spray, but he grasped the oars and plunged them into the seething water. Calling desperately on the power of the golden breastplate, he heaved back with all his might.

The boat lurched, its timbers groaning, water slopping over the stern as Tom brought it to a shuddering halt. Korvax corkscrewed in the air, shrieking in anger and beating her wings furiously. But the magic strength surged through Tom's limbs, giving him the power he needed to drag the struggling dragon back towards the shore.

"Keep it up!" cried Petra.

Tom focused on his rowing, aware that Elenna was doubling the knots that held the rope to the frame of the boat. Even with the power of the breastplate, Tom's muscles burned with the effort. Sweat poured into his eyes and his sinews stretched to breaking point. Vax gripped the sides, his eyes wide as he stared at the thrashing dragon.

It's working!

Gritting his teeth, Tom dug deep. He could see Korvax struggling, the sea dragon's body writhing as she fought to get free. And there, on her flank, Tom saw Simeon's frozen body.

Will we be able to melt him free? Is he even alive?

"We're almost there," shouted Petra.

Tom glanced over his shoulder and saw the shoreline coming closer.

"Tom, look!" yelled Elenna. "Something's happening!" Korvax's tail was melting, and the small frozen creatures encased in the ice were splashing into the water. The rope holding the Beast passed through the melting tail like a hot knife through butter.

"No!" Tom let out a cry of dismay as the lasso fell away and the boat jolted dangerously forwards, almost tipping over. Korvax, now without her tail, dived headlong into the sea, sending up a huge fountain of water that surged over the bows, drenching them all.

The boat rocked wildly for a few moments then became still.

Tom wiped ice out of his eyes. The water calmed. Silence hung over the sea.

Tom hung his head over the oars, panting. "How do we fight a Beast that can melt parts of its body away at will?" he said.

Elenna stared down into the dark water. "She's coming back!" she yelled, jumping back.

The sea dragon surged out of the water, up into the air. Her tail had re-formed into a long spiny whip. It flicked, smacking into the boat. The small vessel flipped, and Tom plunged into the freezing sea, the terrible cold tightening like icy bands around his ribs.

Tom gripped his shield. The power of Nanook's bell would save him from freezing to death.

But what about Elenna and the others?

CLAWS OF THE SEA DRAGON

Tom kicked hard, heading for the light shimmering above him. He fought his way up, the cold clutching his chest and squeezing his lungs.

His head broke the surface and he sucked in air, staring round for the boat's crew. Not far away, he saw

Vax clambering up onto a tipping shelf of ice, floating on the water. Petra was already there, helping him up.

Where's Elenna? Tom twisted his head, hoping to spot his loyal companion. But he couldn't see her anywhere. "Elenna!"

He filled his lungs and dived down, hunting under the upturned boat, hoping she might be in a pocket of air.

There was no sign of her.

He clawed his way down through the dark water, kicking with all his might. He stared out into the gloom, heart thundering and blood ringing in his ears. *What if Korvax has already got—*

He glimpsed a dark shape slowly sinking below him. He powered down, ignoring the agony in his lungs.

It was Elenna – pale as a ghost, her eyes closed and her limbs hanging limply.

Dead? No! I won't believe that.

Tom cut down through the water, driven by sheer willpower, reaching out for her. His numbed fingers closed around her collar. He twisted in the water and kicked for the surface.

They broke into the air. Relief flooded Tom's heart when he heard Elenna coughing, as he dragged her towards the ice floe.

Petra and Vax knelt on the bobbing edge of the ice-shelf. They reached down and pulled Elenna out of the water.

"Make sure she's all right," said Tom. He was about to haul himself up when he heard a screech behind him.

He spun around. Korvax was hurtling through the water towards him, sending up a great churning wake. Her jaws gaped, revealing jutting teeth.

I'm not going to be another meal for you!

Tom whirled away from the platform of ice and ploughed

through the water, arms flailing and legs kicking. Even underwater, his ears rang with Korvax's shrieks.

He turned. Her open mouth loomed like a yawning cavern.

"No!" He thrust his shield between the gaping jaws. The fangs crashed down on it, the wooden edges jamming between the needle-sharp teeth.

Korvax's eyes blazed with anger as she tried to pull free. But Tom shoved the shield deeper into her mouth, locking the jaws open as he struggled to draw his sword.

Korvax shook her head fiercely and Tom's arm slipped from the shield's strap. The Beast dived, his shield still caught between her teeth.

Tom trod water, his heart hammering. Without the warming power of Nanook's bell, the cold gripped him tight.

The dragon's tail reared suddenly out of the sea, curling around and then smashing down. An explosion of water drove Tom under the surface. He tumbled over and over, feeling the cold cramping his muscles and slowing his blood. His vision blurred, and he knew he was about to pass out.

He felt something catch his wrist, then haul him up. Elenna and Vax leaned over him, dragging him out of the water. He struggled to his feet on the ice floe, life stirring in him again. "Korvax?" he said with a gasp.

"She's gone," said Elenna. "But we're a long way from the shore. I don't think we'd survive if we tried to swim."

"And we have no fire," said Vax. "How shall we hold off the sea dragon when she returns?"

Petra was standing on the edge of the floe, her arms wrapped around herself, staring towards land.

"Petra?" Tom called. "Can you make fire by magic?"

The witch didn't respond.

Is she frozen by fear? Or has she lost all hope?

Tom was about to repeat his question when the waters erupted and the sea dragon powered into the air.

Korvax rose high above the floe,

then twisted in mid-air and came crashing down, her talons raking the ice. The floe bucked and spun, a large chunk breaking off under the attack.

"Keep together!" cried Tom, trying to keep his balance.

The Beast rose and dived again, thumping into the ice.

"He's here!" Petra yelled suddenly, pointing.

Tom turned. Rourke was flying towards them, a flaming torch gripped in his claws.

Rourke released the torch and Tom snatched it out of the air. The heat of the flames warmed his body. Korvax dived at them again, but Tom jabbed the torch at her. With a muffled cry, the Beast darted away in a flurry of wings and a flick of her long tail.

Tom stood with his feet spaced

wide apart on the rocking ice. Korvax circled them warily, her eyes on the torch.

"We're safe so long as the torch stays alight," Tom said.

"We're stranded in the middle of the sea!" cried Petra.

"Korvax won't come close while we have fire," added Elenna.

"But we must rescue Simeon!" shouted Vax.

Tom knew they had to lure Korvax closer without giving up the only weapon they had against her.

It's the fear of melting that keeps the Beast at bay. What if we could have heat without fire?

"I have an idea," he said. He held

his sword in the flames, watching as the metal gradually heated up. The hilt became warm in his hand as the blade glowed red.

"What are you playing at?" cried Petra. "We're all about to die, and you're warming your sword up?"

Ignoring her, Tom moved to the lip of the ice-shelf. With a flick of his wrist, he flung the torch into the sea. It lay on the surface, a small flame still flickering.

"Are you mad?" shouted Vax.

"Wait," Tom said. He turned and called out. "Korvax!"

The Beast's rose above the grey waves, wings flapping steadily.

She thinks we're helpless.

Tom stepped back, raising his sword as Korvax dived at the ice floe, eyes glittering with victory.

UNDEFEATED!

Tom braced himself on the ice, his eyes fixed on the Beast and the hot sword gripped in his fist. As Korvax rushed in, he could see his shield wedged between her back teeth.

"Keep back!" he called to the others.

Jets of icy breath spouted from the Beast's nostrils as she dived, claws reaching forwards, eyes filled with cold hatred.

I have to time this right.

As he felt the wind of her wings in his face, Tom flexed his legs. At the last possible moment, just before

the long talons would have pierced him, he sidestepped and swung his sword. He scored a long wound along Korvax's flank, spraying splinters of ice.

With a shriek of pain, the dragon

faltered, one wing hammering down on the ice floe.

But even as Tom thrust his sword again, Korvax recovered, heaving herself into the air. He ducked as her whipping tail swept across the rocking floe. The dragon flapped her spiny wings, powering away.

I can't let that happen! Tom loped across the ice and, judging the moment to perfection, he leaped. The power of the golden boots sent him soaring high. He landed on Korvax's slippery back.

The dragon twisted in the air, trying to throw him off. Tom's feet skidded on the icy scales and he slid sideways, grabbing one of the barbed fins along her spine. It was freezing, and he fought the urge to snatch his hand away. But he held on, enduring the pain and numbness, scrabbling on the scales. He managed to pull himself up on to the ridge of her backbone.

The dragon was rushing headlong into the sky. Tom saw the mist-shrouded sea below, the faces of his companions just dots on the tiny ice floe.

Korvax writhed under him, desperate to shake him loose. But he had a firm grip now, and he moved from spike to spike, climbing towards her neck.

Tom sensed the terrible fury of the

dragon through his red jewel. She twisted her head, trying to snap at him, but the shield stopped her from biting down. Gripping the fin at the base of her neck, Tom leaned to one side, raising his sword and bringing it down. The hot blade cut into the joint of the dragon's wing.

With a hiss, steam clouded from the wound as the blade bit deep. Tom raised the sword and struck again, hitting the same point.

The wing broke away in a blizzard of ice fragments. Korvax gave a shriek of rage, her body tilting to the side, her legs flailing at the air as the severed wing spiralled down to the sea. Tom was almost

wrenched off her back as she twisted downwards, unable to fly straight, her one wing frantically beating the air.

Korvax's eyes bulged with rage, her breath pumping ice into Tom's face. He swung around the spine and swiped the flat of the blade across her eyes. Steam clouded up and a flood of melted ice poured over her eyes. Blinded, Korvax plummeted downwards.

Tom barely hung on. In desperation he thrust his sword deep into her back, gripping hard with both hands as the sea dragon flailed under him.

He stared in alarm as the sea raced up to meet him, the Beast falling backwards. But then, at the last moment, the sea dragon flipped over, crashing belly-first into the waves. Tom was almost ripped off, but managed to keep hold of the hilt of his sword. The Beast skimmed through the shallows then ploughed on to the shore. Shingle and sand sprayed up as Korvax skidded towards the cliffs.

Tom leaped free, leaving his sword wedged in the Beast's back. He landed hard, curling into a forward roll, tumbling along the beach. The Beast hammered into the cliffs with a mighty crash, bringing down huge chunks of snow on to the sand.

Tom got to his feet, dazed and bruised. Korvax lay against the rock, writhing and thrashing her one wing.

Tom stepped forward cautiously. The Beast was down, but was she defeated? He'd only taken a few paces when splinters of ice sprouted out from her shoulder, forming

fins that stretched and flexed. Tom stopped, staring in horror. *Korvax's wing is growing back!* He had no weapon or shield, and he felt exhausted from the fight.

The air shimmered and cruel laughter echoed in Tom's ears. With a swirl of his long cloak, Jezrin appeared in front of him. The wizard smiled. "You cannot defeat Korvax," he said with a sneer. "All you have done is to make her more angry."

"I'll find a way to stop her!" Tom cried.

"Where is your shield?" demanded the wizard. "Where is your sword? Both are gone, and Korvax grows in power and fury. You will die on this beach, boy, and nothing you can do will prevent it!"

Even as the terrible words rang in Tom's ears, the sea dragon reared up behind the wizard, her wings spreading and her eyes fixed on Tom.

1

ICE AND FIRE

Jezrin stepped aside as the Beast stamped forward, talons clawing the ground and wings spanning out. Tom backed off, searching for something he could use as a weapon.

He crouched, ready to dodge, but the Beast's tail flicked forwards and struck his legs, tripping him.

Tom hit the ground, gasping. Before he was able to recover, Korvax was upon him. Her huge claw crashed down on his chest, pinning him to the sand. Tom tried to wriggle away, panic coursing through him. He

couldn't move. The Beast's thirst for blood entered his mind through his red jewel. Her breath surrounded him, freezing his skin. Tom saw with relief that his shield was still wedged in the dragon's mouth and stopping her from closing her jaws. The dragon's foot bore down harder.

I can still be crushed, though. The talons squeezed the breath out of Tom's body. He could hear Jezrin cackling.

"Do you feel your bones breaking, boy? Do you feel the blood congeal like ice under your skin? This is your final Quest. You are— Aargh!" The wizard's rant ended abruptly, with a groan of pain.

Then Tom heard shouting and the thud of running feet. He twisted his head to the side. A host of lizard-people were racing along the beach, crying out and wielding blazing torches. Jezrin lay on the ground, and beside him Nordo stood clutching a small rock.

Tom's spirits soared. Despite their fears, the people had come to his rescue. Korvax lifted her head, an uncertain growl reverberating in her throat, alarm in her shifting eyes.

The dragon's foot lifted and Tom was able to suck in a breath.

The reptile-folk surrounded the Beast, thrusting their torches at her as she cowered back against the cliffs, screeching and flailing her wings. A torch was flung into the Beast's face. With a piercing scream, Korvax reared up on her hind legs, clawing the air with her talons. Tom scrambled clear, taking a torch and sweeping it under Korvax's head.

The Beast fell back, ice-water flooding down her flanks.

"More fire!" shouted Tom, leading the reptile-folk as they crowded around the melting Beast. Korvax's panicked shrieks weakened. The wings drooped, cracked and fell into pools of icy slush.

The body of Simeon slithered down from the dwindling flank of the Beast and the people let out a shout of joy. Two men pulled him away from the thrashing Beast and a woman flung a blanket around him.

Korvax still had the shape of a dragon, but she had shrunk to about

half her previous size. Steaming water poured off her, soaking into the sand. The reptile-folk closed in, thrusting the torches. Soon the Beast was no bigger than a cart; then only the size of a horse, whimpering, pressing against the cliff. At last

she was as small as a flapping chicken. Tom gave one final thrust of his torch and her body fell apart, leaving only a formless lump of ice in the wet sand, no bigger than a man's fist.

"Thank you!" Tom cried, smiling at the people gathered around him.

"You are welcome," said Nordo, taking Tom's hand. "You fought Korvax and rescued Simeon. We are in your debt."

Tom saw that the boy was on his feet now, his face blue with cold as a weeping woman hugged him tight. Torches were held close, warming him. He had survived the terrible ordeal.

Tom stooped to pick up his sword and shield, lying in the meltwater that was all that remained of the Beast.

He noticed something lodged in the face of the shield. He turned it over, looking more closely.

It was the broken end of a fang

from Korvax's mouth.

"Nice work bringing the dragon down!" said a familiar voice. Tom turned and grinned at Petra, who was coming up the beach with Vax and Elenna.

Elenna peered at the fang. "Why hasn't it melted?" she asked.

"That's obvious," said Petra. "It's like Quarg's horn. Full of magic!"

Nordo approached, dragging a cloaked figure behind him. It was Jezrin, looking dazed and embittered, a red lump on his forehead.

"What would you have us do with him?" Vax asked.

Jezrin drew himself up haughtily.

"You will do nothing with me, fool!" The wizard gave the fang in Tom's shield a look of curiosity, then stared into Tom's face. "Release me or face my wrath!"

Tom pointed his sword at the grimacing wizard. "We're taking you back to Avantia," he said. "You will be judged for your crimes and King Hugo will pass sentence on you!"

"It's the dungeons for you, Jezzie!" said Petra, grinning. "I hope you like cockroach soup. It's the best item on the menu. I should know!"

Jezrin drew himself up, his face seething. "I will return to Avantia," he spat. "But on my own terms! Once I have drunk deep from the

Well of Power!" He glared at Tom. "And it will be Hugo who will know the taste of dungeon food! For the brief time before I have him executed!"

"We will never let that happen," said Elenna.

Jezrin's eyes blazed. He twisted in Nordo's grip, swirling his cloak about him. Tom lunged for the wizard but he was too late. In a flash of blue light Jezrin was gone. Nordo stumbled forwards and a murmur of alarm rose from the crowd.

Tom frowned, angry with himself letting the Evil Wizard escape. "Have no fear," he said. "He won't be back. Cowards always run away."

"And I suppose we have to go after him?" grumbled Petra. "While there's blood in our veins...blah, blah, blah."

Elenna smiled. "We'll make a Quester of you yet."

Tom raised his sword and looked towards the cliffs, wondering what dangers lay beyond. "We're not going anywhere until we've rid this kingdom of Jezrin," he cried. "And it doesn't matter how many dragons he throws in our path!"

THE END

1

CONGRATULATIONS, YOU HAVE COMPLETED THIS QUEST!

At the end of each chapter you were awarded a special gold coin. The QUEST in this book was worth an amazing 8 coins.

Look at the Beast Quest totem picture inside the back cover of this book to see how far you've come in your journey to become

MASTER OF THE BEASTS.

The more books you read, the more coins you will collect!

Do you want your own Beast Quest Totem?

1. Cut out and collect the coin below
2. Go to the Beast Quest website
3. Download and print out your totem
4. Add your coin to the totem

www.beastquest.co.uk/totem

8

Don't miss the next exciting Beast Quest book, VETRIX THE POISON DRAGON!

Read on for a sneak peek...

THE TUNNEL OF DOUBT

Icy gusts tore through the drenched fabric of Tom's tunic. He watched the iron-grey waves roll towards him, crashing in a tumble of yellow foam on the white sands of Drakonia. Cold sunlight glanced off the distant swell, making a path of beaten silver from the horizon to the beach. Tom clenched his teeth against the violent shivers that gripped his body, and turned to face the rocky cliffs overshadowing the bay.

Petra and Elenna stood further up the beach, dripping puddles on to the sand. Nearby, the lizard people, wrapped tight in rough-cut furs, were making their way back towards the dark openings of their caves in the cliff face. The gruff but brave Drakonians had just helped Tom, Elenna and Petra defeat Korvax the Sea Dragon – the second Beast Tom had faced since following Jezrin to Drakonia to thwart his evil plan to find the Well of Power.

Tom shoved Korvax's ice fang into his satchel alongside Quarg's stone talon, then trudged to Elenna's side. She turned to him with a tired-looking smile.

"So, what now?" she asked through chattering teeth.

"Home for a warm bath and a hot toddy if we've got any sense," Petra muttered.

Tom shook his head. "Not before we've stopped Jezrin reaching the Well of Power."

Petra rolled her eyes. "You make it sound so simple. But you forgot one tiny detail. *How?* Jezrin's got a head start on us, and since you sent Ferno home, we're stuck without a ride. Not to mention the fact that we don't even know where the well is!"

"The Well of Power!" a young voice cut in. "I know the way!"

Tom looked up to see Simeon, the young lizard boy he had helped rescue from Korvax, starting towards them. Vax, the tall and strongly built leader of the lizard people, caught hold of Simeon's arm.

"Hush, lad," he said. "Tom doesn't want to hear our old folk tales."

"Wait!" Tom said. "Old folk tales have served us well in the past. Let the boy speak."

Vax grimaced, but trudged up the beach to where Tom stood with

Elenna and Petra. Simeon scurried along at his father's side. Tom was glad to see the boy's eyes shining with excitement from under his thick hood. He was clearly none the worse for his time spent frozen inside the sea dragon.

"My old nan says there's a magical passage through the mountains that can lead you close to the Well of Power," Simeon told Tom.

Vax nodded gravely. "It is called the Tunnel of Doubt," he said. "But it's so perilous it was blocked up long ago. The legends say the tunnel drives folk mad, turning brother on brother. All I know is that when people go in, they don't come out."

Petra let out a sigh. "No prizes for guessing where we're headed next then," she said.

Tom ignored the witch. "If Jezrin reaches the Well of Power before us, no one in the known kingdoms will be safe. We'll take the shortcut, whatever the risk."

"Very well," Vax said. "I will lead you there. But beware. Inside the tunnel, your very thoughts will be your enemy."

Tom stood with Elenna and Petra, peering through a dark and jagged cleft between two rocks. His arms ached from hefting rocks and, despite the cold wind, his skin prickled with sweat. Vax had led them around the coast to what looked like an ancient rock fall. After shifting mounds of boulders

and scree aside they had uncovered a narrow entrance leading into the cliff face.

"Good luck,"Vax said, handing Tom a smoking torch. "You're going to need it."Then he turned and strode away.

Tom dipped his head and scrambled through the gap. Inside, a tunnel led away, straight and unbranching, fading quickly into blackness. Smooth stone walls curved to form a ceiling above Tom's head just high enough to walk without stooping. He heard the scrape of boots behind him, and turned to see Elenna squeeze through the gap, followed by Petra.

Rourke, Petra's red crow, hopped through last, his head jerking from side to side as his sharp eyes scanned the tunnel. He let out a squawk, then flapped up on to Petra's shoulder.

Petra stroked the sleek feathers on his neck. "I know," she said glumly. "But at least we're out of the cold."

The air in the tunnel was stiflingly warm, muggy and stale, in a way that made Tom's chest feel heavy with dread.

"Let's get going, then!" Elenna said, with a brightness that didn't match her grim expression.

The three friends set off into the darkness, the crackle of the torch and thud of their footsteps strangely muffled by the dead air. Either side of them bobbing shadows climbed the walls, bent and strange like twisted monsters.

Read

VETRIX THE POISON DRAGON

to find out what happens next!

Fight the Beasts, Fear the Magic

Do you want to know more about BEAST QUEST? Then join our Quest Club!

Visit www.beastquest.co.uk/club and sign up today!

Are you a collector of the Beast Quest Cards? Visit the website for further information.

MEET TEAM HERO
THEIR GIFTS MAKE THEM DIFFERENT
NICE HANDS!
FREAK!
BUT WHEN DANGER COMES...
CRACK!
RUMBLE!
SCREEECH!
...A HERO IS BORN
OTHERS WITH GIFTS WILL SEEK THEM OUT...
...AND SHOW THEM THEIR DESTINY.
EVER HEARD OF HERO ACADEMY?
COMING SOON FROM ADAM BLADE
ADAM BLADE
TEAM HERO
TEAMHEROBOOKS.CO.UK
DARE TO BE DIFFERENT